BOUNDLESS

(STORIES)

SHASHI PATHAK

Dedicated

To

my dear father

Mr. Chandrapal Sharma 'Rasik Hathrasi'

Mrs. Shashi Pathak

Contents

Preface

Women writers have their places in Hindi literature since the beginning of genre of story writing. The first writer of modern story in Hindi was Rajendra Bala Ghosh. She wrote under the pseudonym 'Bang Mahila'and she became famous by this name. although the colour of modernity revealed in her story "Kumbh Mein Chhoti Bahu" published in 'Saraswati' had already been highlighted in 'Madhav Prasad Misha's' story 'Vishwas ka phal' published in 'Sudarshan' in 1901, but 'Kumbh Mein Chhoti Bahu' proved a step in the history of Hindi literature, from where started a new journey of Hindi stories. The ingredients of this story- Village, rural families, the pedantic relation between men and women, master and labour relations and their economic disparities etc.. were highlighted after a decade by Munshi PremChand, at a wider range, in his stories.

It is quite evident that literary skill of women writers is firmly placed like a foundation stone in the field of story writing. A famous story of 'Bang Mahila', 'DulaiWali', published in 'Saraswati' in 1907 was declared as the first fundamental story in Hindi by some writers of history of Hindi literature. This story can also be set to be the first best regional story.

In addition to 'Bang Mahila' one more very reputed writer's story 'Bawli Bahu Ki Veerangana' was published in January month in 1912 in the magazine 'Grah Laxmi' and 'Sacchi Saheli' written by 'Saraswati Devi' was published in 'Grah Laxmi' in October month in 1912.

Tradition of story writing by women writers started in 1922, when publication of magazines like 'Chand' and 'Madhuri' had started seeing the interest and intellect of women. Some notable names in this series are- Shivrani Premchand, Banlata Devi, Hemant Kumari Chaudhrani, Smt. Janki Devi, Mishra Mahila, Kumayun Mahila etc... Some of the women writers who were prominent from 1930 to 1940 are- Usha Devi Mishra, Satyavati Mallik, Kamla Chaudhary, Subhadra Kumari Chauhan, Sumitra Kumari Sinha, Leela Avasthi and Chandra Kiran Sonreksa. Some successful stories of 1950 are- 'SangrahKadiyan Toot Gayin, Pyasi Dharti Sookhe Taal' and 'Moorkh' written by 'Kanchan Lata Sabbarwal' and 'Cigarette ke Tukde' and 'Prem Chunariya Bahurangi' by 'Rajni Panikkar' are the successful story collection on creative values.

Somveera, Shivani, Shashi Prabha Shastri, Vijay Chauhan, Krishna Sobati, Mrinal Pandey, Mridula Garg, Usha Priyamvada and Mannu Bhandari are some other reputed writers of this decade. Except Somveera all the other writers continued to benefit the society with their stories till next four decades. These women writers were not limited in their themes of homely affairs, rather we find a wider range of theme in their writings. Along with the variety of themes like- changing aspect of family relations, break ups of the couple, love triangle, adultery etc, their creations also seem to reveal some new dimensions. During the 70s and after that International Women's Movement has also played its role in the awakening of women conscience.

Today once again we find women writers actively struggling to make their identity in the society of intolerant men critics. Malti Joshi, Deepti Khandelwal, Manjul Bhagat, Krishna Agnihotri, Suryabala, NirupamaSevati, MehrunnishaParwez, Indubali, SimmiHarshita, Namita Singh, Meera Man Singh, Chandra Kanta, Dr. Sarla Agrawal, Dr. Kamal Kumar, Dr. Pramila Verma, Dr. Santosh

Srivastava, Dr. Sarojini Kulshreshtha and the writer of this story collection, Smt. Shashi Pathak are in the list of such writers. In the writings of these writers we find the theme of family disparities in the modern times and the depleting human values, in a modern colour. No doubt their disappointment and hopelessness is evident in their writings but in most of these writings we find a courage to win over these problems. This is an optimistic aspect.

'Boundless' the second story collection of Smt. Shashi Pathak is before you, after making a special place among the women writers with her first story collection 'Fragrance of Relationships'. Stories, short stories, Children's literature of Smt. Shashi Pathak has been published in reputed magazines since last two decades. Besides her Children's novel 'Nikhil aur Grahon ki Anokhi duniya' has been published and collection of short stories 'Kadam Kadam Samjhaute' edited by her has also been published. Her creations have been welcomed in the world of Hindi literature. The present collection 'Infinite' is a high level story collection the writer. It very well reveals that the writer is well experienced and creative. The stories in this collection are full of variety and reveals various dimensions of life's reality. Today man is too much depressed by the disparities in his life and man has become inhumane. All these issues have been covered in this collection. On the one hand there are stories disclosing hollow social relations and on the other hand materialism and human selfishness. Some stories present positivity of human sensitivity. In short, the writer has shown her interest in truth, godliness and beauty of her creativity and had preserved it in her stories in a harmonious way.

The writer has selected the title of the collection on the basis of her strongest story of this collection 'Boundless'.

This is a superior story of positivity. The protagonist of this story 'Poonam Didi' is a very sensitive lady who had been attached to children since the beginning. But after marriage, she did not have any child, so she adopted a child.That also did not live long. Then she started a school for children and showered an infinite love on the children studying in her school. Along with the interest the story gives the message of breadth of love to the readers. Loftiness of this story is also revealed in- Characterization, development of plot, dialogue and impressiveness.

The stories of infinite deal with the disparities of the age on different level. Some of the stories take the readers to life struggle in the present society and compels to think about it.

In the story 'Day dream' the protagonist 'Ranjana' is misguided due to her ambitious nature and suffers. The bad result of her suffering gives us a message. The story 'Tanya' brings out the family problem of a working lady in a patriarchal society and also presents its solution with confidence. 'Faultless' is also a story of women problem in which the story ends happily due to transformation of male member of the family. stories like 'Bet with Destiny' and 'Waiting' also present the breaking relationship as a result of greed of money, selfishness and disappearing human sensitivities.

In the story 'Bet with Destiny' an illiterate woman of rich family is turned out of her house by her brother-in-law and has to lead a life of beggar. The story presents its lively description which gives us a message of 'Adult Education'. The story 'Wait' is a special message to women community. This story provides a positive attitude towards girls who are educated and in job but are having a negative attitude towards married life.

The story 'Alarm' presents a high-level patriotic spirit of an Indian woman, who is the widow of a martyr, comes to murder her own son in a confusion that he is a traitor, but anyhow he escapes death. At the end of story, she is found embracing her son, when he is proved innocent. Through this story, writer has given a unique message of patriotism through brave wives and mothers.

The story 'Dawn' breaks the illusion of the Indian society about the anti-social nature of the foreign wives of migrated boys of Indian families and develops a positive attitude towards them. The story 'The Bond' is of true love of brother-sister who have no blood relation.

In this way we find that different stories of this collection present various problems of life from various angles and along with entertainment they impart a message also. The writer is alert in dialogue construction too. Dialogues are concise, sharp and help in developing a character.

Summing up, the stories of infinite are such as reveal the truth of human life in which the reader realises his own moments of suffering. These stories not only present the problems but also have tried to find a solution to it. All the stories have good moral values. I am quite confident that this collection will be highly accepted in the world of Hindi literature. I congratulate the writer Smt. Shashi Pathak for this collection.

Dr. Anil Gahlot
Reader and Research Director
Hindi Department
K.R [P.G] College. Mathura

Acknowledgements

<u>ON WRITER'S BEHALF</u>

An established scholar is selected for writing the preface to study the writings of the writer and present his/her impartial view before the readers. And from 'The writer's pen' present the feelings and obligations of the writer himself. But this story collection 'Boundless' is such in which the writer was unable to write from her pen by herself due to some painful condition. Hence these few lines are written by myself, her husband, on her behalf.

It was only a coincidence that me and Shashi both had interest in literature even before marriage and our stories had been published in various magazines. After our marriage was fixed, we came to know of this common interest and became each other's complement. We used to be the first audience of each other's creation and tried to make an improvement by giving impartial opinions to each other and we used to send it for publication or for relay from Aakashvani only after improving the matter. This process continued for 18 years. In the meantime, we had two sons. They too were matured enough and started writing stories, short stories and Haiku and started participating in our discussions.

Meanwhile my eight original books and edited books were published and two original and one edited book of Shashi published. But suddenly everything in life turned upside down. 10th November 2000 came as dark day in my life. Returning from office in evening, I found my wife 'Shashi' in desperate condition. She had lost the ability of writing, reading and speaking. Since that day my series of visits to the doctors- Neuro physicians, Vaidya, Speech therapist, and neuro surgeons has not stopped.

Since the last two and half years both of my sons have assisted me in all the household works and how many times I have absorbed the tears of wet eyes of Shashi silently, whenever she wanted to say something but was unable to speak, I am unable to say and my pen does not have power to express this deep sorrow. I don't even know, till when I have to bear this sorrow silently.

Consequently, I collected different compositions of Shashi, that had already been published and relayed fromAakashvani, and decided to get this collection published under the title 'Boundless'. My friend and senior writer Dr. Jagdeesh Vyom, Kamlesh Bhatt Kamal, Muneesh Madir, Madan Mohan Upendra, Dr. Anil Gahlot etc. empowered my thoughts. This collection is of only 64 pages, which can be said to be very brief but I would like to draw readers attention more towards my emotions to get the broken series of her creative writings and get it published. Success of this story collection in the field of Hindi story writing will no doubt be done by the intellectual readers, but as a story writer I am quite sure that stories of this collection will certainly contribute to elevate the respect of Smt. Shashi Pathak, reputed reviewer, Gazal writer, Dr. Gahlot has written its preface. I am heartily thankful to him for this. I will like to extend my obligation to Sri NeerajKaraiya of Karaiya Publication who took the responsibility of publishing this collection. Last but not the least I would like to thank Smt. Vandana Asthana for translating the collection into English. With special regards to the contributors in the field of Hindi Literatureand intellectuals and Kind hearted readers.

Yours

Dinesh Pathak 'Shashi'

ACKNOWLEDGEMENTS

28, Sarang Vihar, Mathura-281006
Mbl-9870631805

CHAPTER ONE

DAY DREAM

The series of Sanjana's thoughts also caught acceleration with the increase in the speed of train. The widespread greenery outside the window was also unable to pacify the chaos going on in her mind. Although her eyes were towards the beautiful scenes outside the window but actually, she was unconscious about it and was sunk deep in her thoughts. Each incident of her life was stinking her mind.

How does one get into someone's captivity talk? Where sometimes does all human conscience go? And he deliberately pushes himself into the abyss of dark!

What to say of others, when Ranjana, who considered herself very smart, gets caught in Sudhir's speech trap.

Sudhir's entry in her life was not so unexpected, but she got trapped in his clever talks in a way that she could not even judge when her heart got out of her control.

She was quite happy to see the double story large building when she reached her in-laws house after marriage. the more amusing was the deep affection that she got from her in-laws. Brother and sister-in-law always lingered around her calling her Bhabhi-Bhabhi. Her husband Rajendra had joked saying, "Have some grace on me also or you will shower all your love on brother and sister-in-law. Her face blushed and showed her thumb towards her husband.

How one month passed after marriage, she could not understand. One day her father-in-law called her. She got terrified. She thought if she had committed any mistake? She tried to recall all her activities from morning till evening, but she could not remember anything that could be her mistake. Thinking over it, she reached before him, with bowed head, shekept standing there hitting the ground with her toe.

Seeing Ranjana standing with hesitation, he laughed loudly.

"Why are you shivering? I have not called you for any of your mistake. I just wanted to ask something."

She shuffled more than before and started thinking about what he wanted to ask me. There was a premonition of fear. She collected courage and looked up hesitatingly.

"Yes father."

"I just wanted to ask, if you want to continue your education. Form filling up is going on, if you are interested, I will ask Rajendra to bring a form for you."

Hearing this, she got crazy with excitement. She felt that she has got everything without asking for it. A moment before she was trembling to come before him and now, just opposite feeling. Her dream of higher studies had shattered when her parents had refused her to continue her studies and married her.

Considering the economic condition of her family. she became ready for marriage. But today she became so happy hearing his words she moved forward and touched his feet.

"Father, I am very much interested in studies. I will continue my studies."

"That's good! All your family members, your sister-in-law, brother-in-law and mother-in-law are highly educated. You also must improve your qualifications. It is a matter of joy for us."

She was provided a separate study room, and she could read whereever she wanted.

After her graduation, she filled form of postgraduation, then B.ed and then, M.ed. in the meantime, there was vacancy in a college, she applied with permission of in-laws and by the grace of God, she was selected. Now she had responsibility of home, as well as college.

After sometime, she gave birth to a child. It filled the whole house with joy. There was a poetry recitation competition in her college. For which she had to prepare students of her class and she herself had to recite a poem. She had interest in poetry writing since college time. Many of her poems had been published in many magazines. She decided to get a few of those poems prepared by the students of her class.

When students recited her poems on the stage, everyone praised it. When she herself recited her self-composed poem, the whole auditorium erupted in applause. She was returning home, overjoyed. The clapping in the hall, still echoing in her ears. She had walked only some distance, when a car came and stopped beside her. She frankly denied to the request of the young man in the car for lift.

"No, I will go on my foot."

"Perhaps you didn't recognise me. I am Sudhir, childhood friend of your husband. I am very much impressed with the poem that you recited. It is your own composition? Presentation was really excellent. You will earn a name in 'poetry conference'.

Sudhir was speaking and she was listening to her praise happily and unmindfully she sat in the car. Feeling happy on her own admiration is perhaps the biggest weakness of a lady.

Since that day, Sudhir's visit to meet Ranjana became very regular. Ranjana too started taking interest in his impressive personality and talks. Now coming and going to college by his car became very regular for her.

With the effort of Sudhir, she got a place among the reputed poets on stage. She got a lot of admiration. After sometime, it became her source of earning too. This changed her direction of thought.

In the beginning, she used to go for participation with the permission of her in-laws, but later she forgot this culture also. She started giving more importance to Sudhir, than her husband. His personality and richness attracted her. She stopped caring for the respect and limitation of the family and the flattery of people attracted her attention more than anything.

Consequently the glare of the stage put a veil on her wit. She lost the sense of right and wrong. And one day the daydream shown to her by Sudhir took her to Mumbai. Her songs were to be recorded for films. Many of Sudhir's friends used to come to his house like directors, producers etc.. Everyone listened to her song, praised it and then-

But man does not listen to the voice of the conscience and remains cheating himself. The black shadow of daydream had already enslaved Ranjana.

One day Sudhir organised a party. In the morning when she got up, her whole body was paining badly. She called Sudhir, but there was nobody in the house. In no time, she understood everything. She was deceived.

Now it was intolerable for her to stay there for even a single moment. She summoned strength with a great difficulty and having reached the station, she took a train to Bhopal.

How she got trapped, Inspite of being educated. How could she forget that third person's interference poisons the relation of husband and wife. Why did she avoid her in-laws and simple-hearted husband. Now she wanted to regret for it. She wanted to reach home at an earliest and beg excuse from everyone.

The fast-moving train too seemed her very slow.

CHAPTER TWO

WAITING

I stopped there only, hearing the conversation inside the room. Whatever I heard was incredible. Did I sacrifice those golden years for this day.

"Listen, till when she would remain dependent on us?"

"Who? Muktadidi? Don't know. She never thinks herself."

The conversation of brother and sister-in-law stirred my conscience like a storm. I had also my own life and family! I was feeling angry over my own decision. So many nice proposals came for me! At least brother knows every situation, we have faced since childhood. How small he was when father had left us crying. We three were left in the world. I had to take the responsibility of the whole family. still he did not give any reply to Bhabhi. He was listening to her silently and gave his consent also.

Why did he do like this? But what may be the obligation that he heard such words for her own sister. I felt all my labour going waste. I was in intermediate when father left us alone in this world. I studied along with job.

Sumit was in third standard then I had to take care his studies too. Since morning I had to get busy in household works. From mother's medicine to Sumit's school and then again evening chores. With all this, my office. This became my daily routine.

In discharge of my duties for the family I forgot myself, my future. The handicapped mother was unaware of the growing age of her daughter. Whenever the neighbours asked about her marriage, she did not take interest and shifted it to them only and I could not say anything. I too realized that after my marriage, the problems of the family will be deepened, so I also kept avoiding my growing age.

I had developed a sort of liking for my classmate, Abhay and he too liked me. When I told him about marriage, he became overjoyed and spoke, "Oh! You just snatched my words. Tell me when are you planning to marriage?"

"Not now. Let me finish my responsibilities, would you be able to wait till then?"

"Yes, why not. But you can do these things even after marriage."

"No Abhay, it will be injustice with you and your family."

"Recently you are alone to carry on the responsibilities, but after marriage both of us will do it together."

"No Abhay, let me do it myself."

"Ok, as you wish, but it would have been better if you............................"

Many years passed. Several times Abhay discussed about it but I was determined to move further in life only after being free from my responsibilities. At last Abhay too became silent. He stopped talking to me on this matter.

After sometime I heard that he got married. I felt restless for some days but then everything became normal and life moved on. I was growing older and now I had stopped thinking about marriage.

After brother's marriage I felt a bit relaxed. All my friends got married and had children too. They always used to come to meet me, whenever they came here, I felt a pain in my heart whenever I met them. All this was natural feminine quality, but I always kept my feelings buried in my heart. It was never revealed on my face.

"Sister, is my lunchbox ready? I am getting late for office."

"Yes it is ready." His voice broke my thought series..

Their conversation was still stirring my mind. But it was morning time. Sumit was going to office. If I said anything, he would be disturbed. I will also remain in tension. Hence I thought it better to keep silent.

As I reached office, peon informed me that boss had called me. I asked, "Why?"

"I don't know madam."

I went to his cabin. He was on a phone call. After he kept the receiver I asked, "May I come in sir?"

"Yes, have your seat."

"You had called me sir."

"Yes, you have been promoted. You have to go to Faridabad."

"When sir?" I asked curiously.

I was happy but when I told this to everyone at home, they looked depressed, but no one opened his mouth.

Then time came when I had to go. I sat in train. Sumit touched my feet. I had a strange feeling while blessing him. I thought that he was doing all this only to show otherwise he would not have supported his wife that day.

On the way to Faridabad, I kept thinking about Sumit and his wife, childhood time of Sumit. I recalled the day when I had to stay in office and Sumit was very restless without me , he did not even eat anything. I had promised him that I would never stay in office till late hours. But everything had changed with time. Now Sumit has no time for me. And it's alright. He is grown up now. He must walk alone. He is capable today, but I have become incapable.

Today, Abhay is coming to my mind again and again. If I had responded to him that time, my condition would not have been so miserable. But it's no use to cry over the spilt milk. I became conscious as soon as the train stopped with a jerk.

I looked out of the window, the station had not yet come. After sometime the train started and the train reached the station. I picked my suitcase and alighted on the station.

Taking out the address written on paper and enquired the location and took a rikshaw. I reached my friend's house in sector 27. She was over joyed to see me and hugged me warmly. We had tea and gossiped. I asked her about Abhay. She informed that Abhay was married and had two children.

Her answer made me dull but tried to give strength to my mind. I thought what was his fault. I alone was responsible for hid condition of mine. That time I was busy in earning for my family. I had never thought that everyone will change with time. For whom I sacrificed my life will also not care for me.

"What are you thinking?"

"Nothing."

"How far is office from this place?" I asked just to change the topic.

"2-3 km."

"Can we easily get vehicle from here?"

"Yes."

The next morning I reached the office and was shocked to read the name on the name plate outside the chamber. Then the second thought came, it might be some other person, then again the thought came, if it were the same Abhay, how would she face it? But why should she trouble herself, he is already married.

With all these thoughts I entered the room.

"Come, Miss Mukta."

He told in a tone as if he had been waiting for me only. I was sure now that it was some other person, not Abhay.

"What are you thinking Miss Mukta?"

"Nothing sir."

Now I saw my boss intently. Again and again my mind was going towards Abhay. I wish Abhay were my present boss! I started thinking again.

"Miss Mukta, your immediate boss is out of station for 3 months. I have been given this charge. So, I am explaining you your work."

"Sir, may I get a glass of water?"

I requested with a dry throat.

"Why not?" and he asked the servant to bring a glass of water.

It was two months, since I had joined this office. I was busy in files, when receptionist called me, saying someone had come to meet me.

I went to the reception hall and found Sumit there.

"How? Sumit, what happened?"

"I want some money."

"Oh! But for what?"

"Actually sister, Prabha wants to buy a car."

"That's good. Why don't you purchase?"

"But we don't have enough money. If you help me with 50-60 thousand rupees...."

"I can't arrange so much money. Whatever I had I spent on you all. Money doesn't grow on trees that I will pluck and give it to you."

That day's harsh words of Sumit and his wife came to my mind and my tone became harsh.

"Prabha was telling about your provident fund."

I thought today I am their sister. That day they forgot everything, my every obligation when Prabha was denoting me as a burden and wanted that I should leave the house . now she wants some money from my provident fund!

I thought all these things but did not reveal that I had heard their conversation that day. But this was the only reason I tried for transfer and came to Faridabad. I only said, "It's not easy to withdraw the money from P.F in my department."

Hearing this Sumit looked disappointed and went away without saying anything. I came back home and lied down on my bed as if there was no energy in my body. I was in a state of confusion- on the one hand my angry feelings for Sumit and his wife due to their mistreatment, on the other hand the disappointed face of Sumit when he went away from here. My ego prompted me not to help Sumit, while my heart said something else.

"What will I do with the money? For whom I am collecting it? None but Sumit will use this money after me. I have already sacrificed my life for him. Then why to think so much now. Let him enjoy all the luxuries of life. I had myself chosen this path of thorns, rejecting Abhay's proposal. Abhay is also married. Then wait for whom now? Who will marry me at this declining age. So let me apply for the money. Let Sumit enjoy.Some people are born to lead a luxurious life while some are born to suffer.

"Madam, sir is calling you."

It was the peon of this new office. I got up immediately and reached his cabin.

"May I come in sir?" I asked for permission.

"Yes come in." he answered while attending a call. I exclaimed with a hidden joy, "Abhay!"

It was no one but her own Abay on the chair of manager. Shewas feeling a strange joy that she was unable to express, but the next moment I thought that I should remain unaffected as Abhay is married now and he has children too, so it doesn't matter whether it is my Abhay or someone else.

"You!" Abhay was shocked as he saw me after keeping the receiver.

"Yes sir, I was transferred here, when you were abroad. In these three months, I always kept thinking, if it was you or some other Abhay."

"And after three months, you found the same Abhay!" he laughed heartily in his same old style. I came out of my dream and said, sir you had called?"

"Yes, tale your seat Mukta. How is everyone at home?"

"Sir, I enquired about you in Sumit's marriage but could find you nowhere."

"Yes, I was abroad for my engineering."

"I had heard this news and also that you married there and have two children."

He laughed again loudly in the same familiar style. Then became silent and asked, "What about you? have you become free from your responsibilities or are there some still remaining?"

Now I am free. Sumit has got job and is married. He is busy with his family. Mother is no more." I told with a deep sigh and drop of tears came in the corner of my eyes and throat chocked.

"Why have you applied for withdrawing money from your P.F then? What's the problem?"

"Actually, Sumit needs money, not me. He had come here at first, I thought of not helping him. Then I thought what will I do with the money. There is no colour in my life. At last, all I have will go to him only. That's why I thought of withdrawing the money. By the way Abhay, I did a great injustice to you by not obeying you, but now it's no use to cry over the spilt milk. Leave it. Tell me how your wife and children are?"

Once more he laughed loudly and said, "Whom are you talking about, Mukta. I am still waiting for you."

"What?" I exclaimed.

"Yes Mukta."

"But my friend told me..........."

"She must be joking."

I thanked God but remained silently.

"What are you thinking, Mukta? Any more responsibility?"

Both of us laughed loud.

"No, Abhay................."

CHAPTER THREE

BET OF DESTINY

"Mother! where are tea leaves?" I was surprised. Rahul is asking for tea leaves but he never drinks tea. I thought and asked from inside the bathroom.

"Why do you need it?"

"Tell me soon. I have to prepare tea."

"It is there in bottle of coffee, in the glass almirah of the lower shelf. How did you feel like drinking tea today? Any friend has come?"

"No mummy, you come out first."

By the time I came out, Rahul's school bus had come. He picked up the bag and said running.

"Mother, an old woman is sitting outside. Give her the tea. I have poured it in the cup."

I came out with tea cup, after Rahul went to school, but found no one. Amit, a boy of neighbourhood was preparing for going to school. I asked him, "Amit, did you see any old woman here?"

"Which old woman aunty? Are you talking about Elizabeth?"

"I don't know the name. but Rahul had told me to give tea to an old woman sitting outside."

"Sure. She must be Elizabeth. A very carefree woman. Goes anywhere she wants and eats anywhere she gets to eat. But aunty, her clothes and stick are lying here. She must be around here. But why are you asking?"

"No dear. Rahul had prepared tea for her but his school van had come, so he left for school immediately and asked me to give her the tea."

I was about to turn and come inside, when I saw the old woman in rags. But her clothes were clean and hair tidy. She did not at all look mad. She seemed to be a lady from some respectable family.

Taking the tea cup from my hand, she moved towards the tree and sat under it. I too came inside and got busy in my daily works, but there was something in her face and eyes that I kept thinking about her. I felt that I have seen her somewhere, but was not able to recall. Again and again her blank eyes seem familiar to me and was attracting me.

I tried to recall, but was unable to remember. Then I thought, must have seen her begging somewhere and tried to put away the thought but my thoughts kept lingering around that Elizabeth.

I came in the drawing room and started reading the newspaper when suddenly a news attracted my attention. I started reading the news and I remembered everything that I was trying to recall. Every incident of 15 years before became alive in my memory. He was transferred to Jhansi. We did not get government quarter, so we lived on rent in the house of Mr. Ashok Garg. They had no child, so Mrs. Garg used to come to me after finishing her work and we used to gossip for a long time. She treated me as her younger sister.

Once my husband had gone out of station for some official work. It was night and raining heavily. There was heavy lightening too. I was suffering from heavy pain. When I could not tolerate, I called Mrs. Garg. Both husband

and wife took me to the hospital in a taxi and after two to three hours, Rahul was born.

Mr Garg and his wife were busy in their own world. They always enjoyed their life unconcerned about the world outside. But after the birth of Rahul, they got busy with Rahul, as if they had got a toy to play. With a little cry of Rahul, they came running.

Time was passing. Rahul had become three years old. I was transferred to Mathura. When we started from Jhansi, Mr. and Mrs. Garg became very sad. They took Rahul on their lap and their eyes became wet. They kissed Rahul again and again. Our correspondence continued even after we came to Mathura. But slowly it became irregular and then extinct.

One day a headline in the newspaper caught sight. "Businessman of Jhansi, Sri Ashok Garg, murdered. Murderers fled." I became speechless when I read the news. When we reached Jhansi, we were informed that Mrs. Garg had gone to her village.

The ring of call bell brought me out of deep thought. Coming out I saw Elizabeth coming with the tea cup. She was mummering something and extended the empty cup towards me.

"What's your real name, Elizabeth?" I enquired her taking the cup in my hand.

She looked at me and started weeping, "My name is unfortunate."

"Unfortunate? Why?"

"There is no better name for me than unfortunate. What I have? Nothing- I have lost everything- Husband, home, shop, otherwise I would not have been wondering like a beggar today."

I became more curious and asked her to tell her story in detail.

"What will you do sister, listening to my sorrowful story?"

"I was full of sympathy for her. I said, "Life is full of ups and downs. But how did you reach this condition Inspite of wealth, shop, home etc....... I want to know."

She felt comfortable with my words and stared into my face and don't know why she started crying loudly. I thought she had recalled something or had recognised me. Is she the same lady as I am thinking? She embraced me and called me Kusum. I too became emotional. Just then my husband entered and stopped for a moment, seeing me embracing a beggar. Before he could say anything, I spoke out.

"Do you remember Rohit, 15 years before, we lived on rent in Mr. Ashok Garg's house. later on he was murdered. She is the same Rajnididi."

"Rajni Bhabhi! How did you come in this condition?" Taking her to the drawing room, Rohit asked.

With our affection, she started expressing her supressed feelings.

"After my husband's death, my brother-in-law supported me for sometime, but later I realised that it was all due to selfishness. He got my signature on a blank paper and grabbed my property, house, shop and everything. Mr. Garg always used to say to me to learn reading and writing. But I always neglected. I remained illiterate and suffering for that."

"Did you not file a case against him?"

"Signing on a blank paper, I myself lost my right on everything. How could I file a case? And it is very necessary to be educated to fight a case. That's why I thought of leaving everything. After all everything will be theirs only after my death."

"But, how did you come in such condition?"

"He was not satisfied even after this. He made a conspiracy against me to kill me, so that the problem is finished from the root. But I guessed his conspiracy and ran away from there in the dark of night. There was no one left after my parent's death, so no question of going there. therefore I sat in the train going to Mathura to take refuge in the feet of lord Krishna." She started looking at me helplessly.

By the grace of God, you have come here, sister-in-law. Now you see how I will deal with them. You stay here comfortably. It's your house only.

CHAPTER FOUR

THE BOND

I was very happy to receive Barkha's letter. It mentioned, "We are coming by Chhattisgarh Express on 10th." The letter gave me a great joy and I started waiting for the 10th date.

On 10th I became ready very early in the morning and instructing Aradhana, what to prepare, I left for the station to receive them. On the way to the station, I was thinking about the days, I had spent with Barkha. Every memory moved like a reel.

Ours and Barkha's family were very intimate. Our affection for each other was an example for everyone. Barkha was the only child of her parents and I too.

I always longed for a sister and that I got after getting Barkha. We had an emotional relationship and started sharing even small things between us.

Our families were also very closely attached. Since childhood Barkha and I used to play and go to school together. She always keep on calling me for even small matters.

Our parents were overjoyed to see our affection. They were happy that we got each other's company. We even used to stay at each other's home. Our parents used to say that our relation was of prior birth.

Once I had an attack of typhoid. Barkha never let me alone. All were worried about health. She used to pray God for my recovery.

"O God! Please relieve my brother from suffering."

After I recovered, she wept bitterly clinging to me and said, "Never do this gain otherwise your sister will die."

"Crazy girl! It's not depending on us. Nothing can happen to my sister." I patted her lovingly. Our parents became emotional seeing our affection. But our neighbours started doubting our pure relation. They started the hard blow of society on this pure relation.

Now ours every activity was looked with suspicion. One day Barkha's cycle broke by being struck to a scooter and she went with me to school for two to three days. Everything turned into a storm. People started taunting me.

"There is no relation of brother and sister between them. They have wrong relation."

I felt angry and told Barkha to go by rikshaw to escape useless talks of people.

But she immediately denied and said, "Why should I go by rikshaw? I shall go with my brother. People are like dogs, let them bark. Our relation is pure. Why should I fear?"

Our parents too came to know about these rumours but they did not pay attention to it as they had full faith on us.

But an incident affected Barkha's parents badly. Some people had came to see Barkha for marriage. neighbours told wrongly about our relation. They went away declaring Barkha as characterless.

Then only I realised that the pure childhood love is taken in a wrong way when we grow up.

Barkha's parents too were so much affected by these rumours as it became difficult to get her married. So one day they announced, "Dear Rohit, we know that even a real brother can't give so much love and protection to Barkha as she got from you, but society never understands this. We too are a part of society. We can't remain aloof from the society. So my son please save my Barkha from these rumours."

That day was very sorrowful and restless for me. I could not concentrate myself. Once I thought of marrying Barkha but the next moment my conscience rebuked me. I had always seen her as my sister. How can I even think about it? I have to find some other way. Sunk in these thoughts, the whole night passed.

In the morning, it was too late when I was awoken by mother, "Get up Rohit see who has come."

I came to the drawing room yawning and was overjoyed to see my friend Amit after along time.

"Oh! Amit! You were on training?"

"Yes, I was on training. But mother suddenly fell ill and I had to come back immediately."

Just then mother came with fritters and tea and said, "Amit, this hot water, wash your hands and face and have your breakfast."

"Mother is suffering from high blood pressure. She wants that I should get married. Just tell dear, is it so easy."

"Hmm.. that's why you are here. You have come to meet me or to ask someone's address."

"You started joking yarr.. I have come only to meet you. We have met after a long time."

"Yes it's true." Suddenly I recalled Barkha and I became serious.

"What happened Rohit? Why have you become serious?"

"Nothing dear, suddenly I recalled a girl who can solve your mother's problem. But I am thoughtful whether to tell you or not. You too are a part of this society."

"Why are you talking in riddles? Tell me who is the girl?"

"That girl is my sister Barkha but many rumours are spread in the society about our relation in a wrong way. People are trying to blame our pure relation. So, nobody is ready to marry Barkha. In such a situation I can't expect anything from you."

"Are you talking of the same Barkha who was very intimate to you and was not tired of calling you 'Rohit Bhaiya'."

"Yes, you're right."

"I am ready to marry your sister."

"Really Amit! Even after knowing these things about her!" my eyes became full of tears and could not speak anything being overjoyed.

"Yes Rohit, I don't care for the society. I have full faith on my friend. I will marry Barkha."

"Rohitbhaiya! Rohitbhaiya!" called Barkha and came out of my deep thought. I was filled with joy to see Barkha, Amit and their lovely son.

CHAPTER FIVE

BOUNDLESS

"Oh, Raju! Gudiya! Where from did you get these water guns?" I asked seeing the new water guns in their hands.

Taking out colour from his pocket of his trousers, Raju said.

An aunty lives in the fourth house from here. She had organised anAntakshari competition among we children and gave this water gun to the children who won and these colours too.

A strange feeling started to emerge in my mind as I heard Raju's words and moved back in my childhood. About 35 years before when we lived in Meerut, There lived Poonam didi in my neighbourhood. On the day of Holi, she used put colour on everyone's face and distributed sweets. Then she used to make groups of children and we had antakshari competition the party which won was given the water gun and colours of different variety. Then she was married. Her husband was a supervisor in a company in Dehradun. She rarely came to Meerut, but could never come on Holi. We remembered her very much on Holi.

After sometime, father was transferred to Roorkie and we all went with him. I started thinking about the person who had given these children colours and water gun. May be she is Poonam didi or someone else.

"What are you thinking mummy? I am very hungry." Raju's voice broke the silence and brought me out of my deep thought.

"Nothing........." I stammered as if I have been caught stealing by someone. I collected more information about that lady while serving them food.

"How does she look? What must be her age?"

"What do you mean by how does she look? She is nice looking. About 50 or 55 years." Raju said eating food.

50 to 55 years! Might be she is our Poonam didi! There was a black mole on her chin.

"Is there a black mole on her chin?" I asked unmindfully.

"Oh mummy! You must be in C.I.D. she has given us something, not taken from us. Why are you so much worried?"

Both started laughing. They perhaps can not understand my attachment to Poonam didi. And so many memories of those days.

Next day reached her home after finishing my household work. A middle- aged woman opened the door. I went inside and sat on sofa and started thinking, what should I talk? Just then the lady asked, "What's your name?"

"Madhuri, and yours?" I too asked.

"Revati." She answered.

I became dull. She is not that lady. She is someone else. Perhaps on Holi she too....

Just then someone called from inside, "Revati, who is there on the door?"

"Madhuri madam has come. I could easily guess that Revati was her servant. After a few moments, the lady who came out, really shocked me. I stood there with folded hands.

"Who are you dear? I couldn't recognize you."

"How will you recognize me. When we met, I was very small. We met mostly on Holi. Do you remember Mr. Sharma in Meerut? I am his daughter only."

She tried to recall and said, "Oh, yes, I remember, you are the same Madhuri who used to sing very sweetly? How are you?"

She asked embracing me.

"Everything is fine. Seeing colours and water guns in children's hand I remembered you. I can't tell you how happy I am to see you!" I said being emotional.

"Revati bring some snacks- Gujhiya and Mathri for Madhuri."

After some time, Revati came with snacks and keeping it on table, she went away. We got busy in gossiping.

"Didi, I have got chance of meeting you on Holi for the first time after your marriage. where had you been for such a long time?"

I used to visit Meerut, but you were not there." She said looking at me.

"Yes, father was transferred to Roorkie. Brother completed his engeneering from there only. And I was married just after doing B.A. I have two children- Raju and Gudiya. How many children you have, didi?"

She sighed heavily and said, "I have no child, Madhuri." Her eyes had become wet.

I felt very bad. I thought why I asked her about her children and hurt her. I felt angry on God. Why he did not give her children. She loves children. Children loving lady is craving for a child.

"Why didn't you adopt a child from orphanage?"

She became more emotional.

"Yes dear, I had adopted a new born child. I brought him up lying awake the whole night. He grew up. He started going to school. But God snatched him from me one day." Telling this, she started crying.

I consoled her, "What can we do before God's will?"

"Yes, it's true dear. Tell me how are you?"

"I am ok didi. My husband is a doctor. My children you have already met. How do you live in such a big house?

"Today is holiday. Otherwise this house resonates with screams of the children. I brought this big house after retirement. We have kept two rooms for ourselves and in the remaining we run school. My husband and I run this school. We remain busy in it. Time passes easily."

"Grandmother, we have brought the vegetables you had asked to bring." Two boys came inside and kept bags before her.

Then came two other boys and hung on her neck saying, "what are you doing grandmother?"

Didi embraced him and patted his head.

I feltthat her personality had become boundless.

CHAPTER SIX

TANYA

Alighting from the train on station, Tanya cast her eyes in all directions, but could not find any known person. Has her life become so strange? Tanya gave a thought and started thinking about her past. She was thinking that if she was happy in past or now? He was moving ahead thinking when rikshaw rider called her, "Where you have to go, madam?"

She asked surprisingly, "will you go to Radhika Vihar?"

Without waiting for his reply she kept her luggage in the rikshaw. Her memories were moving ahead with the rikshaw.

She was the eldest amongst the three sisters. The most beautiful of the three. She was slim, with long hairs and sharp features. Though she was not much qualified, she had a deep desire of making a progress.

Father always remained worried about marriage of his three daughters because of their fast growing age.

Mother always used to convince him, "Why do you worry? Someone will marry my daughters one day without dowry."

"Do you know what type of proposals come without dowry- either there is some problem with boy or in family."

One day father was very happy when he returned from the office. he said, "You were right. Today I have got a very nice proposal for Tanya. There is no demand of dowry. The boy is cashier in bank. His first wife died one year before."

"Then he must have two to three………"

"No, he has no child." Father understood mother's mind before she spoke out. "Our Tanya will be very happy there."

Preparation of marriage started and like other girls Tanya also came to her husband's house with dreams.

She got everyone's love in her in-laws house. time was passing happily. She continued her study with their permission. One year passed. One day, she suddenly fell sick. Consulting the doctor it was found that she was pregnant. She was very happy. Her exams were going on. She was hesitating to think how she would go to give exam in such condition.

Some day after exam, Palak was born. She was overjoyed to see that healthy and beautiful daughter. Her mother-in-law also got busy with Palak and was happy.

With her own efforts and the support of mother-in-law, she completed her B.A and B.ed. After that she joined a school near her home.

One day, she was sitting quietly when someone knocked the door. as soon as she opened the door, a stranger was standing before her. He had an interrogation on his face.

"Excuse me, my niece studies in your class. She told that you had called me."

"What's the name of your niece?"

"Ragini."

"Oh you are the uncle of Ragini."

"How did you call me?"

"You have to be careful about her studies. She may fail in maths."

"What should I do mam? Can you take her tuition?" he told sensing her.

Hiding her feelings, she said, "I don't have time but can find some time in evening."

"O.k., she will come in the evening from tomorrow."

"She got some other tuitions along with Ragini. Her economic conditions improved and along with it her feelings too changed. Now she started insisting her husband, Vinayak to live separate from his parents. The issue became a cause of their day to day quarrel. Finally his parents themselves convinced him to arrange a separate house as per his wife's wish.

Her greed of money was increasing day by day. She always lived in wants, so now she wanted to buy her joys with money. Now reaching home late became routine of her. It disturbed her married life. Conflict between husband and wife became very common and neighbours started spreading rumours. One day as soon as Tanya entered, she heard a loud cry of child. "Now you have come after enjoying yourself. See how bitterly she is crying! Don't you have any care for her."

Picking up the child and embracing her Tanya said, "Maid was in the house."

She got frightened when Vinayak said in harsh voice, "You don't know this also. Maid has not come today."

Just then the rikshaw stopped with a jerk and she too came out of her thoughts. Perhaps some child had come before the vehicle. The rikshaw driver continued grumbling and scolding the boy.

" Leave it man. We have not yet covered even half distance. Still a long way to go."

She told a rikshaw driver and told him to move ahead. Same things started moving in her mind again.

Since that day Tanya had become more revolting and revengeful. The more Vinayak scolded and insulted her, the more aggressive she became. The moment she entered her home, rumpus started. She was compelled to tolerate the poisonous words of Vinayak, and used to weep bitterly in the bed.

Palak was also growing up. She had admitted Palak in a nearby school. Several times she thought of leaving job and take care of householdwork but thinking about the economic problem she had to withdraw her decision. But she was deeply hurt due to the increasing doubts and aggressive words of Vinayak.

One day she was shocked to hear what Vinayak was asking to Palak. That day he had crossed all the limits.

"Palak dear, how many uncles come to meet your mother."

That small innocent child could not understand the import of his words and started mentioning the names of all the guardians who used to come- Gupta uncle, Sharma uncle, Yadav uncle and ..."

"Stop it! What are you asking her? Ask me whatever you want." All the softness of behaviour disappeared and she roared like a lioness .

Vinayak spoke louder showing his domination being a male, "I know everything. I don't need to ask anyone about you."

She had a severe headache that night. The following morning she got up late and could not go to school. She thought of taking a leave for at least four days. But it was very difficult to pass even a single day, let alone the thought of living four days in this house. So next day she went to school.

"Why did you not come to school yesterday madam? Are you okay?" asked the principal.

"I was not well sir so I could not come."

"You must take care of your health." He went into his cabin saying this.

In the evening while returning she decided to have a check up in doctor Mathur's clinic. There were not many patients so she went inside.

"Hello Mrs. Tanya. How are you?" doctor asked.

"I was not feeling well so I thought of visiting your clinic."

Doctor Mrs. Mathur appreciated Tanya's decision and said that health should never be neglected. But whatever the doctor told after check up was incredulous.

"Congratulations Tanya! you are pregnant."

"What! What are you saying doctor?"

"Whatever I diagnosed. And it's right time. Your daughter has also grown up now."

She was very quiet that day. When she gave this news to Vinayak his reaction shocked her. She was thinking he would be happy but what ever he told hurt her very deeply, as if someone has poured melted lead in her ears.

"It's not my child? Where from have you brought it?" she could not believe her ears. Vinayak had crossed all limits. How can he be so cheap.

"Shit! I hate him."

A lady can tolerate everything but not doubt on her character.

"What are you saying? Have you thought?"

She broke out in emotion and anger. But he was unaffected and made a satire, "Truth is very hard to digest, isn't it Tanya?"

"Shame on such husband! I always tried to do best for this family. this is result of my sacrifice! And it is no one but my own husband who has blemished my character! He has brought me after taking seven circumambulations around the sacred fire!"

Now it's too much! I should not tolerate any more. She started hating her husband.

She took a firm decision. After admitting Palak in a hostel she filed a case against her husband. Although she knew that this path was also not easy in a patriarchal society. She will have to face many practical problems. But all these difficulties seemed very dwarf before the insult that she had to tolerate every moment.

She felt herself like a bird free to fly as high as she could.

CHAPTER SEVEN

DAWN

I was in a dilemma having received Prabhat's letter. On the one hand the joy of meeting son , daughter in law and grand- daughter and on the other hand the , memory of their first visit started paining my heart.

Every sound at the door, filled me with excitement as if he had come. A strange happiness clouded her mind since she had heard that her children were coming. Time of wait was seeming very long. Today I was going to get the result of my whole life's sacrifice.

Born and brought up in poverty, I always compromised with my desires. Being good at studies. I could continue my studies on scholarship. I wanted to be a doctor and whenever I went to hospital with father and saw doctors on round, in white uniform , my ambition of being a doctor grew stronger. I always determined to be a doctor but being the eldest among brothers and sisters. I could never raise my voice.

The ring of call bell interrupted the series of my thought perhaps he has come. I got up enthusiastically and opened the door. But the milkman at the door ended all my excitement.

" Madam from today the cost of milk has increased by one rupee" he said , pouring milk in the pan. " It's o.k. , but bring more milk from tomorrow."

" Is anyone coming , madam ?"

" Yes, Prabhat is coming."

" It's a very good news !"

I went into the kitchen and put the milk on the gas burner , thinking that my sorrows are going to end. I never got a space in my life since childhood. I always curbed my desires and gradually all my ambitions were buried , except one wish. I tried to fulfil my ambition. Passed the entrance exam too , but suddenly father had a heart attack and then a second attack. I was compelled to drop my ambition and marry , everyone gave me full love and support in my in laws house but my husband everyday come home , heavily drunk. I had to tolerate all those thing I understood why he married such a poor girl like me.

After two to three months, I conceived and giving him an oath in the name of coming child. I requested him to stop drinking and to my amazement he accepted my proposal. I was very happy but my joy was not for a long time. It was raining very heavily I was feeling very peculiar that day. There was a heavy lightning. It became dark but he did not return. I was filled with so many questions. Suddenly the call bell rang.

Opening the door and was shocked to see my husband badly bleeding in the hands of our neighbour , Mr. Ram Nath.

" Sister, my friend has left us forever."

I was speechless and became unconscious. Coming to senses I come to know that he died being crushed under a lorry.

I decided to do something to earn my livelihood. I started stitching clothes and then tuitions. I had to bring up Prabhat. Due to lack of money Prabhat's study too suffered , hence I decided to continue my education. At last I became a lecturer. Now my only aim was to make Prabhat a doctor.

Everything was going accordingly. Prabhat cleared the entrance exam and got admission in the medical college, He got scholarship from government to continue his higher education abroad. I was very happy. My dream was coming true.

A knock at the door , interrupted my thought series.

There was postman at the door, he handed me a telegram. I had a sudden premonition of fear but got relaxed when I read it. It said , "We are reaching India on June 10 in the evening. The clock showed 6.30 p.m.the time was passing. Every moment was seeing very long like ages. Every word in the telegram was arising questions in my mind. But very soon all my anxiety was buried with the message of Prabhat on telephone that he has gone to a hotel , straight from the airport. I reached on the address and looked at Prabhat with a question on my face and responded immediately " maa actually our house is very small. She may face problem , so.."

Yes , the same house where Prabhat was born and brought up was very small for him today. I came back home with heavy heart , thinking that happiness is not in my lot. Husband left , Prabhat is no more my right , all my struggle for nothing. I was lost in thoughts when the call bell at the door interrupted my thoughts. I got up with a start and opened the door. For my surprise it was Prabhat with his wife and baby.

" Oh ! You !"

" Yes mother !" Both touched my feet.

But I was still in a dilemma and asked " Why didn't you make an arrangement for her in the hotel ?"

No , mother , now I will open my clinic here only. See maa ! I have learnt to speak Hindi too. Hindi words from the mouth of a foreign daughter – in – law seemed very sweet. I was overwhelmed with joy and taking my granddaughter in my lap , hugged her.

FAULTLESS

Mother's letter had put me in a dilemma. I was unable to decide what to do. The lines in the letter were emerging like a whirlpool in the mind. The more I read the letter, the more tense I became. I read the letter again.

" Dear son. We have fixed your marriage. Engagement ceremony is on 20th and marriage after 10 days. So take a leave and come soon. "

This was not the first letter on the matter. Two years before also mother had posted me such a letter. It was full of the promise of girl and her family. I was very happy to read it. I was mad with joy. Actually, I was tired of bachelor life and wanted some partner with whom I could share my joys and sorrow.

I had drawn a picture of the girl from the letter of mother and I always dreamt of my life with her. Friends also started making preparation to go in the marriage procession. In the next letter mother sent her photograph. I was crazy she was really very beautiful. I kept her photograph in my wallet and at night under my pillow.

Once my friend Ganesh tried to crack a joke and he took away her photograph from my wallet. I got angry over him. " Why are you so vexed. Only eight days are left. You will meet her in reality." Ganesh commented and handed me the photograph.

I got irritated and said , " Where did you get it ?"

" Under the pillow , when I was giving the bedsheet and pillow cover to the washerman. " And he started for office.

I too packed my suitcase and caught train at eight O'clock and reached home. I was very happy I felt as if every free , beds full of flowers , greenfield rivers all were greeting me joyfully.

At home , everyday , there was some or other ritual. Sisters in law made jokes and at last the day came when I reached her home with the marriage procession.

She came on the stage, looking very beautiful among the flowers with a flower garland in her hand and put it around my neck. I was lost in her beauty my dream broke when my friend pushed me. I too put the garland around her neck. There was a big clapping in the pandal. Then continued many rituals throughout the night.

We reached back to our house. Many relatives were eagerly waiting for the new bride. The whole day was spent in rituals and then came the precious moment to meet my life partner. Unveiling her I saw her beautiful face and was thrilled to see the moonlike beauty and spoke out, " I am blessed to get such a beautiful life partner."

"I am more blessed than you. You are God , you have accepted me Inspite of knowing all the facts about my life "

Her words brought me out of my toxication and asked her , " What ! What facts you are talking of ? I don't know anything about you. Tell me everything clearly."

Poonam was quite afraid to see my changed disguise and with tears in her eyes , she asked surprisingly , " What? you don't know anything about me ? But I was told that you have promised to accept me Inspite of having every information about me."

"Accident ! what accident ? But I am totally unaware of any dark fact about your life."

She narrated all the story of her life , weeping. She told , " I was only two years old. My mother went to visit her suffering sister. The neighbour misbehaved with me. I started crying. The neighbours collected and got that person arrested. I was taken to the hospital in an unconscious state."

Saying all this she looked at me helplessly as if she wanted to ask what her fault was. But I became stone hearted and did not listen to her.

" No , I can't accept you after knowing all these things. I am not a social reformer." saying this I rushed out of the room in anger.

But later I came to know that my parents knew everything about it. But perhaps due to the greed of dowry or three daughters to be married. I don't know why they didn't tell me anything about it. The more I thought the more I was confused.

Poonam never came back to in-law's house again. Though I knew she was innocent , But the fire burning inside my heart burnt all me desires into ashes. Many times, I got seriously ill but never called her. My friend Ganesh tried to convince me many times.

Perhaps I too could never forget her tear full eyes. I always thought where was her fault ? But I was never ready to withdraw. Her parents too come to me pleadingly but I never answered but my anger was against whom ? Was it against Poonam or that culprit neighbour or against the system of society ? I was unable to decide.

But today I received mother's letter for my marriage , the memory of Poonam , became fresh in my mind. Her words -----. "What is my fault ? tell me , what is my fault ? "

started hammering my mind.

The whole night passed without sleep , tossing in the bed. Wherever I tried to sleep her tearful face came before my eyes I became restlessness.

In the morning , with the chirping of birds and rising sun, I left the bed. Being free from daily routine. I become ready and started my journey to bring Poonam back. I sent a wire to mother " Mother , your son will no more wander. He is going to bring his Poonam back."

CHAPTER NINE

ALARM

I got up with the ringing of the alarm. It was only 2 AM. Why at this hour? I myself get up in time everyday. In the company of my husband who is major in army, I have learnt at least discipline if not anything else. He is very punctual. A clock can stop but he can never. I still remember once when I had become late in preparing breakfast he left it and went on his work. Since then I have promised to do all works punctually.

There was no sleep in my eyes. my son was also not there who would have set the alarm. I felt a mild heaviness in my head due to incomplete sleep. I got up. Had a glass of water and lay down again on the bed. It was a new place for me so I could not sleep soundly the whole night.

My eyes became teary as I looked at the photograph of my husband hung on the wall. What a self-confident, radiant and smiling face! It seems as if he would speak just now. On the other wall was the picture of India and his photograph receiving the degree in college. I started staring at his face and sunk deep in thought.

Father was very happy that day when he returned from his office. We all brothers and sisters looked at him when mother asked, "Why major saheb? What's the matter? You are very happy today."

"If you listen, you will also be happy."

"What's the matter? Let us also know."

"I have got a very suitable match for our Kusum."

"Oh! who is he? What does he do? Where does he live?"

"The boy is in army and lives in this town only. I have brought his photograph also."

"The boy is perfect but..............he is in army. We have only one daughter. No I am not ready for this proposal." Mother said looking at the photograph.

"Again you talked like a crazy person. I am too in the army. We can never go against our fate where ever we work or go. Father persuaded mother with his convincing talks.

I was married and came to in-laws house. everyone was very gentle and cooperative. I was sitting hesitatingly when my husband entered the room and seeing towards me he said, "You are really like a fairy from the heaven. You have full right to be my second love."

"Second love!" became suspicious and asked, "Second love means?"

"Got worried? Don't worry. She is not my first first wife. She is our mother India. She is the first love of every true patriot." Saying this he embraced me.

Everything was going on smoothly. Each family member was fully disciplined and patriotic. I got the same environment as was in my parents' house. one day, I discovered that I was pregnant. I was very happy and waiting for him to give this good news just then the telephone bell rang and I picked up the receiver.

"Hello! A patriot speaking. Enemy has attacked our country's border. I have to go to the front. I don't know when I will return. You should not worry."

"Hello! Hello!" I kept on speaking but there was no reply from the other side. He had already kept the receiver. There was a strange silence in the whole house. firing from both sides was not coming to end. Everyone was listening to news on radio and T.V channels and were very frightened. Time was awful. Nothing was in favour.

One day I felt a pain in stomach and was taken to a nursing home. By the next morning our son Bharat was born. Here I gave birth to Bharat and there war ceased. Everyone was feeling relaxed. All the soldiers had come back but wait for my husband was not coming to an end.

One day I was giving bath to Bharat and saying, "Now be a good boy. Father will come and will be happy to see you." Just then hearing the call bell, I rushed towards the door. It was postman with a telegram. Grabbing it in my hand, what I read made me lose my sense, "Major patriot martyred.

Everything was dark before my eyes. I became unconscious and fell on the ground. All the joys scattered within a moment. But I decided to make Bharat a true patriot. Since then I took a great care of his education and cultured behaviour. My son also understood my feelings and moving step by step he became Captain Bharat and is serving the country.

I got conscious with the chirping of birds and milkman's call on the gate. My eyes had turned red due to sleeplessness. I then got busy in my day's work. Just then Bharat came and hung to my neck. "How are you mother? why this reddishness in your eyes?"

"Nothing dear, could not get sleep after 2'o clock."

"Why did you get up at 2'o clock?

"Perhaps you had set alarm. So my sleep got disturbed."

"What? The alarm rang at 2 AM?" looked at me surprisingly.

"Now leave it and have your tea."

He drank the tea without any interest and reached near the clock. As soon as he pressed the button, a voice came , "Juliet speaking."

"Major Bharat here. Why had you called at 2'o clock at night?"

"I don't know. Boss wanted to have a talk with you. Today again, he will call at 3 AM."

"O.K" saying this he switched off the phone and calling out, "Mother" as he turned back he was startled to see me ,thinking I had heard him

"What happened dear? Has the enemy attacked our country?"

"Oh! No mother. there was some other work." He said hesitatingly.

"Oh! I thought there is something wrong. Now come on hot water is ready, have your bath. I am preparing your breakfast."

After having his breakfast, Bharat slept but my mind was still troubled. I thought, what can be relation between alarm and his conversation. May be some secret information that can't be shared through telephone. Today's telephone system is so incredulous. Then I recalled, Bharat's father used to say that many army officers have become traitors and are leaking out many secret messages to foreign spies. No, what I have started thinking? Our country can not do such things. Shaking my head I tried to divert my mind from these thoughts.

But the next moment the thought went back to the same place. Then I was afraid to think, what will happen? Will all my wishes be ruined? will the sacrifice of Bharat's father go waist? No, I will not let it happen. Its true that country is at the first place for me but then.....why will Bharat do like this?

With all these confusions in mind I went to sleep. Sleep was very far but still I was trying to sleep. My heart was pounding, if my doubts come true? Oh god! What is my sin for which you are giving me such a big punishment. Lost my husband at the young age. Now in this old age, Bharat is my only support. But I don't want support of a traitor. He will be my enemy. I will kill him. I don't know when I slept. Just then telephone rang and Bharat spoke from this side, "Hello, Captain Bharat speaking."

"Immediately provide the maps of all your centres and details of your arms and ammunitions."

"When and where?"

"Exactly one hour from now, you will meet our man who will take you to the right place."

"Symbol?"

"Black rose in the coat."

"O.K" saying this Bharat took out some files from the Almirah. As soon as he was about to move, I stood actively and fired at him. Bharat fell down on the ground. I became like a statue and looking at his lifeless body. Suddenly I became affectionate. What have I done? I have myself killed my love. I can not live without Bharat. I will kill myself also. No, never!

I got up terrified after this nightmare. How awful the dream was! This dream has taken away my world! I ran towards Bharat's room. He was busy writing something on table. There were files all around the table. I got a bit relaxed. I saw towards the watch. It was not yet 3'o clock. I took a bottle from the fridge and drank it and asked Bharat also for water.

"Yes mother, give me."

As soon as I kept the glass of water, the clock struck 3. Immediately Bharat switched on the phone and spoke,

"Hello! Captain Bharat speaking."

I tried to listen his conversation in the other room.

"Reach with your luggage within an hour." Received order from the other side."

"Its ok, but take care of my share." With this Bharat switched off his phone, collecting his files and made a move. I got aside so that he might not see me. I was really shocked to hear his conversation. What is it happening? Is it all happening as per my dream? Shall I have to take action? No I can not do this way. But Bharat has become a traitor. I can not let him do this way. With a flash of second, I reached near him, "What are you doing Bharat?"

"Nothing mother, nothing!"

"You are hiding something from me, Bharat. My son, traitors never earn name for them."

"No mother, nothing like this. You are in a confusion."

"Confusion and me? Then what is all this? Secret messages in the alarm clock. Are you deceiving your country?"

"Yes, I am a traitor and will deceive my country."

"How unfortunate I am! Had I given birth to you for this day? But I will not let you do this. I aimed at him taking out my pistol- beware I am wife of patriot. If you try to move out of this room, all the bullets will pierce your body."

But Bharat snatched the pistol from my hands. My head got struck against the wall, it was dark everywhere and I fell down unconscious.

With the first sunshine and chirping of birds I opened my eyes. my head was paining. All the incidents of the previous night started storming my mind. Body had become dull. I was crying within my heart as I could not stop Bharat from betraying. My whole life went in vain.

Call bell was continuously ringing. The boy from neighbourhood, Banti, was shouting, aunty, see, Bharat bhaiya's photo is published in the newspaper.

I got up with support and opened the door and taking the newspaper from his hand I started reading it.

"Wise, young, Captain Bharat has got a triumph over the enemy by, finding out the hidden place of enemies, misguiding them to give the documents without caring for his life."

Tears came into my eyes and felt proud on my son. After sometime a jeep stopped before the door. getting down from the jeep, Bharat fell into my feet and started weeping bitterly, "Mother excuse me for my wrong act of yesterday night. I was bound not to reveal you the reality at that time, because the spies of enemy were keeping an eye on every activity of ours. If I had blurt out the secret by being emotional, I would not have succeeded. Please excuse me mother."

"No my dear son, today you have made me and our country feel proud on you. I had only this expectation from you God bless you my son! son of a patriot."